William Watson

Wordsworth's Grave and Other Poems

William Watson

Wordsworth's Grave and Other Poems

ISBN/EAN: 9783337206895

Printed in Europe, USA, Canada, Australia, Japan

Cover: Foto ©Andreas Hilbeck / pixelio.de

More available books at **www.hansebooks.com**

THE CAMEO SERIES

WORDSWORTH'S
GRAVE
and other Poems

GRASMERE CHURCHYARD.

WORDSWORTH'S GRAVE

and other *Poems*
by
WILLIAM WATSON

CAMEO
SERIES

LONDON
T. FISHER UNWIN
PATERNOSTER SQ
1891

[*Second Edition*]

Note to Second Edition.

TWO pieces printed in the First Edition are here withdrawn. Four others not included in the First Edition are inserted For leave to reprint these latter I thank the Editors of the *Spectator*.

Twenty-seven Epigrams are also included in this edition, besides the twenty printed in the former one.

W. W.

JAMES BROMLEY,

Lathom, Lancashire.

ERE vandal lords with lust of gold accurst
  Deface each hallowed hillside we revere—
Ere cities in their million-throated thirst
  Menace each sacred mere—
Let us give thanks because one nook hath
      been
  Unflooded yet by desecration's wave,
The little churchyard in the valley green
  That holds our Wordsworth's grave.

'Twas there I plucked these elegiac blooms,
  There where he rests 'mid comrades fit and
      few,
And thence I bring this growth of classic
      tombs,
  An offering, friend, to you—
You who have loved like me his simple
      themes,
  Loved his sincere large accent nobly plain,
And loved the land whose mountains and
      whose streams
  Are lovelier for his strain.

It may be that his manly chant, beside
  More dainty numbers, seems a rustic tune ;
It may be, thought has broadened since he
    died
  Upon the century's noon ;
It may be that we can no longer share
  The faith which from his fathers he re-
    ceived ;
It may be that our doom is to despair
  Where he with joy believed ;—

Enough that there is none since risen who
    sings
  A song so gotten of the immediate soul,
So instant from the vital fount of things
  Which is our source and goal ;
And though at touch of later hands there float
  More artful tones than from his lyre he
    drew,
Ages may pass ere trills another note
  So sweet, so great, so true.

Contents.

Wordsworth's Grave.

I.

THE old rude church, with bare, bald tower,
  is here ;
Beneath its shadow high-born Rotha flows ;
Rotha, remembering well who slumbers near,
  And with cool murmur lulling his repose.

Rotha, remembering well who slumbers near.
  His hills, his lakes, his streams are with
    him yet.
Surely the heart that read her own heart clear
  Nature forgets not soon : 'tis we forget.

We that with vagrant soul his fixity
  Have slighted ; faithless, done his deep faith
    wrong ;
Left him for poorer loves, and bowed the knee
  To misbegotten strange new gods of song.

Yet, led by hollow ghost or beckoning elf
　Far from her homestead to the desert
　　bourn,
The vagrant soul returning to herself
　Wearily wise, must needs to him return.

To him and to the powers that with him
　　dwell :—
　Inflowings that divulged not whence they
　　came ;
And that secluded spirit unknowable,
　The mystery we make darker with a name ;

The Somewhat which we name but cannot
　　know,
　Ev'n as we name a star and only see
His quenchless flashings forth, which ever
　　show
　And ever hide him, and which are not he.

II.

Poet who sleepest by this wandering wave !
　When thou wast born, what birth-gift hadst
　　thou then ?
To thee what wealth was that the Immortals
　　gave,
　The wealth thou gavest in thy turn to men ?

Not Milton's keen, translunar music thine ;
  Not Shakspere's cloudless, boundless human
      view ;
Not Shelley's flush of rose on peaks divine ;
  Nor yet the wizard twilight Coleridge knew.

What hadst thou that could make so large
      amends
  For all thou hadst not and thy peers pos-
      sessed,
Motion and fire, swift means to radiant ends ?—
  Thou hadst, for weary feet, the gift of rest.

From Shelley's dazzling glow or thunderous
      haze,
  From Byron's tempest-anger, tempest-mirth,
Men turned to thee and found—not blast and
      blaze,
  Tumult of tottering heavens, but peace on
      earth.

Nor peace that grows by Lethe, scentless
      flower,
  There in white languors to decline and cease ;
But peace whose names are also rapture,
      power,
  Clear sight, and love : for these are parts of
      peace.

III.

I hear it vouched the Muse is with us still ;—
  If less divinely frenzied than of yore,
In lieu of feelings she has wondrous skill
  To simulate emotion felt no more.

Not such the authentic Presence pure, that
      made
  This valley vocal in the great days gone !—
In *his* great days, while yet the spring-time
      played
  About him, and the mighty morning shone.

No word-mosaic artificer, he sang
  A lofty song of lowly weal and dole.
Right from the heart, right to the heart it
      sprang,
  Or from the soul leapt instant to the soul.

He felt the charm of childhood, grace of youth,
  Grandeur of age, insisting to be sung.
The impassioned argument was simple truth
  Half-wondering at its own melodious tongue.

Impassioned ? ay, to the song's ecstatic core !
  But far removed were clangour, storm and
      feud ;
For plenteous health was his, exceeding store
  Of joy, and an impassioned quietude.

IV.

A hundred years ere he to manhood came,
  Song from celestial heights had wandered
    down,
Put off her robe of sunlight, dew and flame,
  And donned a modish dress to charm the
    Town.

Thenceforth she but festooned the porch of
    things ;
  Apt at life's lore, incurious what life meant.
Dextrous of hand, she struck her lute's few
    strings ;
  Ignobly perfect, barrenly content.

Unflushed with ardour and unblanched with
    awe,
  Her lips in profitless derision curled,
She saw with dull emotion—if she saw—
  The vision of the glory of the world.

The human masque she watched, with dream-
    less eyes
  In whose clear shallows lurked no trembling
    shade :
The stars, unkenned by her, might set and rise,
  Unmarked by her, the daisies bloom and fade.

The age grew sated with her sterile wit.
　Herself waxed weary on her loveless
　　throne.
Men felt life's tide, the sweep and surge
　　of it,
　And craved a living voice, a natural tone.

For none the less, though song was but half
　　true,
　The world lay common, one abounding
　　theme.
Man joyed and wept, and fate was ever new,
　And love was sweet, life real, death no
　　dream.

In sad stern verse the rugged scholar-sage
　Bemoaned his toil unvalued, youth un-
　　cheered.
His numbers wore the vesture of the age,
　But, 'neath it beating, the great heart was
　　heard.

From dewy pastures, uplands sweet with
　　thyme,
　A virgin breeze freshened the jaded day.
It wafted Collins' lonely vesper-chime,
　It breathed abroad the frugal note of Gray.

It fluttered here and there, nor swept in vain
    The   dusty   haunts   where   futile   echoes
        dwell,—
Then, in a cadence soft as summer rain,
    And sad from Auburn voiceless, drooped
        and fell.

It drooped and fell, and one 'neath northern
        skies,
    With southern heart, who tilled his father's
        field,
Found Poesy a-dying, bade her rise
    And touch quick nature's hem and go forth
        healed.

On life's broad plain the ploughman's con-
        quering share
    Upturned the fallow lands of truth anew,
And o'er the formal garden's trim parterre
    The peasant's team a ruthless furrow drew.

Bright was his going forth, but clouds ere long
    Whelmed him ; in gloom his radiance set,
        and those
Twin morning stars of the new century's song,
    Those morning stars that sang together,
        rose.

In elvish speech the *Dreamer* told his tale
　Of marvellous oceans swept by fateful
　　wings.—
The *Seer* strayed not from earth's human pale,
　But the mysterious face of common things

He mirrored as the moon in Rydal Mere
　Is mirrored, when the breathless night hangs
　　blue :
Strangely remote she seems and wondrous
　near,
　And by some nameless difference born anew.

V.

Peace—peace—and rest ! Ah, how the lyre is
　loth,
　Or powerless now, to give what all men
　　seek !
Either it deadens with ignoble sloth
　Or deafens with shrill tumult, loudly weak.

Where is the singer whose large notes and
　clear
　Can heal and arm and plenish and sustain ?
Lo, one with empty music floods the ear,
　And one, the heart refreshing, tires the
　　brain.

And idly tuneful, the loquacious throng
    Flutter and twitter, prodigal of time,
And little masters make a toy of song
    Till grave men weary of the sound of
        rhyme.

And some go prankt in faded antique dress,
    Abhorring to be hale and glad and free ;
And some parade a conscious naturalness,
    The scholar's not the child's simplicity.

Enough ;—and wisest who from words for-
    bear.
    The kindly river rails not as it glides ;
And suave and charitable, the winning air
    Chides not at all, or only him who chides.

VI.

Nature ! we storm thine ear with choric
    notes.
    Thou answerest through the calm great
        nights and days,
" Laud me who will : not tuneless are your
    throats ;
    Yet if ye paused I should not miss the
        praise."

We falter, half-rebuked, and sing again.
 We chant thy desertness and haggard gloom
Or with thy splendid wrath inflate the strain,
 Or touch it with thy colour and perfume.

One, his melodious blood aflame for thee,
 Wooed with fierce lust, his hot heart world
  defiled.
One, with the upward eye of infancy,
 Looked in thy face, and felt himself thy
  child.

Thee he approached without distrust or
  dread—
 Beheld thee throned, an awful queen,
  above—
Climbed to thy lap and merely laid his head
 Against thy warm wild heart of mother-
  love.

He heard that vast heart beating—thou didst
  press
 Thy child so close, and lov'dst him unaware.
Thy beauty gladdened him ; yet he scarce less
 Had loved thee, had he never found thee
  fair !

For thou wast not as legendary lands
　　To which with curious eyes and ears we
　　　　roam.
Nor wast thou as a fane mid solemn sands,
　　Where palmers halt at evening.　Thou wast
　　　　home.

And here, at home, still bides he ; but he
　　　　sleeps ;
　　Not to be wakened even at thy word ;
Though we, vague dreamers, dream he some-
　　　　where keeps
　　An ear still open to thy voice still heard,—

Thy voice, as heretofore, about him blown,
　　For ever blown about his silence now ;
Thy voice, though deeper, yet so like his
　　　　own
　　That almost, when he sang, we deemed 'twas
　　　　thou !

VII.

Behind Helm Crag and Silver Howe the sheen
　　Of the retreating day is less and less.
Soon will the lordlier summits, here unseen,
　　Gather the night about their nakedness.

The half-heard bleat of sheep comes from the
    hill.
Faint sounds of childish play are in the air.
The river murmurs past.   All else is still.
    The very graves seem stiller than they were.

Afar though nation be on nation hurled,
    And life with toil and ancient pain de-
      pressed,
Here one may scarce believe the whole wide
    world
    Is not at peace, and all man's heart at rest.

Rest ! 'twas the gift *he* gave ; and peace ! the
    shade
He spread, for spirits fevered with the sun.
To him his bounties are come back—here laid
    In rest, in peace, his labour nobly done.

Ver Tenebrosum.

Ver Tenebrosum:

SONNETS OF MARCH AND APRIL, 1885.

I.

THE SOUDANESE.

THEY wrong'd not us, nor sought 'gainst us
    to wage
  The bitter battle.   On their God they cried
  For succour, deeming justice to abide
In heaven, if banish'd from earth's vicinage.
And when they rose with a gall'd lion's rage,
  We, on the captor's, keeper's, tamer's side,
  We, with the alien tyranny allied,
We bade them back to their Egyptian cage.
Scarce knew they who we were!   A wind of
        blight
  From the mysterious far north-west we came.
Our greatness now their veriest babes have
        learn'd,
  Where, in wild desert homes, by day, by
        night,
Thousands that weep their warriors unreturn'd,
  O England, O my country, curse thy name !

II.

HASHEEN.

"OF British arms, another victory!"
   Triumphant words, through all the land's
      length sped.
   Triumphant words, but, being interpreted,
Words of ill sound, woful as words can be.
Another carnage by the drear Red Sea—
   Another efflux of a sea more red!
   Another bruising of the hapless head
Of a wrong'd people yearning to be free.
Another blot on her great name, who stands
   Confounded, left intolerably alone
   With the dilating spectre of her own
Dark sin, uprisen from yonder spectral sands:
   Penitent more than to herself is known;
England, appall'd by her own crimson hands.

III.

THE ENGLISH DEAD.

GIVE honour to our heroes fall'n, how ill
  Soe'er the cause that bade them forth to die.
  Honour to him, the untimely struck, whom
    high
In place, more high in hope, 'twas fate's harsh
    will
With tedious pain unsplendidly to kill.
  Honour to him, doom'd splendidly to die,
  Child of the city whose foster-child am I,
Who, hotly leading up the ensanguin'd hill
His charging thousand, fell without a word—
  Fell, but shall fall not from our memory.
Also for them let honour's voice be heard
  Who nameless sleep, while dull time
    covereth
With no illustrious shade of laurel tree,
  But with the poppy alone, their deeds and
    death.

IV.

GORDON.

IDLE although our homage be and vain,
  Who loudly through the door of silence press
  And vie in zeal to crown death's nakedness,
Not therefore shall melodious lips refrain
Thy praises, gentlest warrior without stain,
  Denied the happy garland of success,
  Foil'd by dark fate, but glorious none the less,
Greatest of losers, on the lone peak slain
Of Alp-like virtue.   Not to-day, and not
  To-morrow, shall thy spirit's splendour be
Oblivion's victim ; but when God shall find
  All human grandeur among men forgot,
Then only shall the world, grown old and
    blind,
  Cease, in her dotage, to remember Thee.

V.

GORDON (*concluded*).

Arab, Egyptian, English—by the sword
  Cloven, or pierced with spears, or bullet-
    mown—
  In equal fate they sleep: their dust is grown
A portion of the fiery sands abhorred.
And thou, what hast thou, hero, for reward,
  Thou, England's glory and her shame? O'er
    thrown
  Thou liest, unburied, or with grave unknown
As his to whom on Nebo's height the Lord
Showed all the land of Gilead, unto Dan ;
  Judah sea-fringed ; Manasseh and Ephraim ;
And Jericho palmy, to where Zoar lay ;
  And in a valley of Moab buried him,
Over against Beth-Peor, but no man
  Knows of his sepulchre unto this day.

VI.

The True Patriotism.

The ever-lustrous name of patriot
  To no man be denied because he saw
  Wherein his country's wholeness lay the flaw,
Where, on her whiteness, the unseemly blot.
England! thy loyal sons condemn thee.—
    What!
  Shall we be meek who from thine own
    breasts draw
  Our fierceness? Not ev'n *thou* shalt overawe
Us thy proud children nowise basely got.
Be this the measure of our loyalty—
  To feel thee noble and weep thy lapse the
    more.
This truth by thy true servants is confess'd—
  Thy sins, who love thee most, do most
    deplore.
Know thou thy faithful! Best they honour
    thee
  Who honour in thee only what is best.

VII.

Restored Allegiance.

Dark is thy trespass, deep be thy remorse,
 O England! Fittingly thine own feet
  bleed,
 Submissive to the purblind guides that
  lead
Thy weary steps along this rugged course.
Yet . . . when I glance abroad, and track the
  source
 More selfish far, of other nations' deed,
 And mark their tortuous craft, their jealous
  greed,
Their serpent-wisdom or mere soulless force,
Homeward returns my vagrant fealty,
 Crying, "O England, shouldst thou one
  day fall,
Shatter'd in ruins by some Titan foe,
 Justice were thenceforth weaker throughout
  all
The world, and Truth less passionately free,
 And God the poorer for thine overthrow."

VIII.

The Political Luminary.

A skilful leech, so long as we were whole :
    Who scann'd the nation's every outward part,
    But ah ! misheard the beating of its heart.
Sire of huge sorrows, yet erect of soul.
Swift rider with calamity for goal,
    Who, overtasking his equestrian art,
    Unstall'd a steed full willing for the start,
But wondrous hard to curb or to control.
Sometimes we thought he led the people
        forth :
    Anon he seemed to follow where they flew ;
Lord of the golden tongue and smiting eyes ;
    Great out of season, and untimely wise :
A man whose virtue, genius, grandeur, worth,
    Wrought deadlier ill than ages can undo.

IX.

Foreign Menace.

I MARVEL that this land, whereof I claim
　　The glory of sonship—for it *was* erewhile
　　A glory to be sprung of Britain's isle,
Though now it well-nigh more resembles
　　　　shame—
I marvel that this land with heart so tame
　　Can brook the northern insolence and guile.
　　But most it angers me, to think how vile
Art thou, how base, from whom the insult
　　　　came,
Unwieldly laggard, many an age behind
　　Thy sister Powers, in brain and conscience
　　　　both ;
In recognition of man's widening mind
　　And flexile adaptation to its growth :
Brute bulk, that bearest on thy back, half
　　　　loth,
　　One wretched man, most pitied of mankind.

X.

Home-Rootedness.

I cannot boast myself cosmopolite ;
   I own to "insularity," although
   'Tis fall'n from fashion, as full well I know.
For somehow, being a plain and simple
     wight,
I am skin-deep a child of the new light,
   But chiefly am mere Englishman below,
   Of island-fostering ; and can hate a foe,
And trust my kin before the Muscovite.
Whom shall I trust if not my kin ? And whom
   Account so near in natural bonds as these
Born of my mother England's mighty womb,
   Nursed on my mother England's mighty
     knees,
And lull'd as I was lull'd in glory and gloom
   With cradle-song of her protecting seas ?

XI.

Our Eastern Treasure.

In cobwebb'd corners dusty and dim I hear
A thin voice pipingly revived of late,
Which saith our India is a cumbrous weight,
An idle decoration, bought too dear.
The wiser world contemns not gorgeous gear ;
Just pride is no mean factor in a State ;
The sense of greatness keeps a nation great ;
And mighty they who mighty can appear.
It may be that if hands of greed could steal
From England's grasp the envied orient prize,
This tide of gold would flood her still as now :
But were she the same England, made to
feel
A brightness gone from out those starry eyes,
A splendour from that constellated brow ?

XII.

REPORTED CONCESSIONS.

So we must palter, falter, cringe, and shrink,
  And when the bully threatens, crouch or
    fly.—
  There are who tell me with a shuddering
    eye
That war's red cup is Satan's chosen drink.
Who shall gainsay them?   Verily I do
    think
  War is as hateful almost, and well-nigh
  As ghastly, as this terrible Peace whereby
We halt for ever on the crater's brink
  And feed the wind with phrases, while we
    know
There gapes at hand the infernal precipice
  O'er which a gossamer bridge of words we
    throw,
Yet cannot choose but hear from the abyss
The sulphurous gloom's unfathomable hiss
  And simmering lava's subterranean flow.

XIII.

Nightmare.

(Written during apparent imminence of war.)

In a false dream I saw the Foe prevail.
  The war was ended ; the last smoke had
    rolled
  Away : and we, erewhile the strong and
    bold,
Stood broken, humbled, withered, weak and
    pale,
And moan'd, " Our greatness is become a tale
  To tell our children's babes when we are
    old.
  They shall put by their playthings to be
    told
How England once, before the years of bale,
  Throned above trembling, puissant, gran-
    diose, calm,
  Held Asia's richest jewel in her palm ;
And with unnumbered isles barbaric, she
  The broad hem of her glistering robe im-
    pearl'd ;
  Then, when she wound her arms about the
    world,
And had for vassal the obsequious sea."

XIV.

LAST WORD: TO THE COLONIES.

BROTHERS beyond the Atlantic's loud expanse ;
   And you that rear the innumerable fleece
   Far southward 'mid the ocean named of
      peace ;
Britons that past the Indian wave advance
Our name and spirit and world-predominance ;
   And you our kin that reap the earth's
      increase
   Where crawls that long-backed mountain
      till it cease
Crown'd with the headland of bright esper-
      ance :—
Remote compatriots wheresoe'er ye dwell,
   By your prompt voices ringing clear and
      true
We know that with our England all is well :
   Young is she yet, her world-task but begun !
By you we know her safe, and know by you
   Her veins are million but her heart is one.

Miscellaneous Sonnets, Lyrics, &c.

Mensis Lacrimarum.

(MARCH, 1885.)

M ARCH, that comes roaring, maned, with
       rampant paws
    And bleatingly withdraws ;
March,—'tis the year's fantastic nondescript,
    That, born when frost hath nipped
The shivering fields, or tempest scarred the
       hills,
    Dies crowned with daffodils
The month of the renewal of the earth
    By mingled death and birth :
But, England ! in this latest of thy years
    Call it—the Month of Tears.

In Laleham Churchyard.

(AUGUST 18, 1890.)

'TWAS at this season, year by year,
   The singer who lies songless here
Was wont to woo a less austere,
   Less deep repose,
Where Rotha to Winandermere
   Unresting flows,—

Flows through a land where torrents call
To far-off torrents as they fall,
And mountains in their cloudy pall
   Keep ghostly state,
And Nature makes majestical
   Man's lowliest fate.

There, 'mid the August glow, still came
He of the twice-illustrious name,
The loud impertinence of fame
   Not loth to flee—
Not loth with brooks and fells to claim
   Fraternity.

Linked with his happy youthful lot,
Is Loughrigg, then, at last forgot ?
Nor silent peak nor dalesman's cot
.. Looks on his grave.
Lulled by the Thames he sleeps, and not
By Rotha's wave.

'Tis fittest thus ! for though with skill
He sang of beck and tarn and ghyll,
The deep, authentic mountain-thrill
Ne'er shook his page !
Somewhat of worldling mingled still
With bard and sage.

And 'twere less meet for him to lie
Guarded by summits lone and high
That traffic with the eternal sky,
And hear, unawed,
The everlasting fingers ply
The loom of God, .

Than, in this hamlet of the plain,
A less sublime repose to gain,
Where Nature, genial and urbane,
To man defers,
Yielding to us the right to reign,
Which yet is hers.

And nigh to where his bones abide,
The Thames with its unruffled tide
Seems like his genius typified,—
  Its strength, its grace,
Its lucid gleam, its sober pride,
  Its tranquil pace.

But ah ! not his the eventual fate
Which doth the journeying wave await—
Doomed to resign its limpid state
  And quickly grow
Turbid as passion, dark as hate,
  And wide as woe.

Rather, it may be, over-much
He shunned the common stain and smutch,
From soilure of ignoble touch
  Too grandly free,
Too loftily secure in such
  Cold purity.

But he preserved from chance control
The fortress of his 'stablisht soul ;
In all things sought to see the Whole ;
  Brooked no disguise ;
And set his heart upon the goal,
  Not on the prize.

With those Elect he shall survive
Who seem not to compete or strive,
Yet with the foremost still arrive,
      Prevailing still :
Spirits with whom the stars connive
      To work their will.

And ye, the baffled many, who,
Dejected, from afar off view
The easily victorious few
      Of calm renown,—
Have ye not your sad glory too,
      And mournful crown ?

Great is the facile conqueror ;
Yet haply he, who, wounded sore,
Breathless, unhorsed, all covered o'er
      With blood and sweat,
Sinks foiled, but fighting evermore
      Is greater yet.

The Mock Self.

FEW friends are mine, though many wights
    there be
Who, meeting oft a phantasm that makes
    claim
To be myself, and hath my face and name,
And whose thin fraud I wink at privily,
Account this light impostor very me.
What boots it undeceive them, and proclaim
Myself myself, and whelm this cheat with
    shame ?
I care not, so he leave my true self free,
Impose not on me also ; but alas !
I too, at fault, bewildered, sometimes take
Him for myself, and far from mine own sight,
Torpid, indifferent, doth mine own self pass ;
And yet anon leaps suddenly awake,
And spurns the gibbering mime into the night.

˙Life without Health.

BEHOLD life builded as a goodly house
  And grown a mansion ruinous
With winter blowing through its crumbling
    walls !
The master paceth up and down his halls,
And in the empty hours
Can hear the tottering of his towers
And tremor of their bases underground.
And oft he starts and looks around
At creaking of a distant door
Or echo of his footfall on the floor,
Thinking it may be one whom he awaits
And hath for many days awaited,
Coming to lead him through the mouldering
    gates
Out somewhere, from his home dilapidated.

On Exaggerated Deference to Foreign Literary Opinion.

WHAT ! and shall *we*, with such submissive
    airs
As age demands in reverence from the young,
Await these crumbs of praise from Europe
    flung,
And doubt of our own greatness till it bears
The signet of your Goethes or Voltaires ?
We who alone in latter times have sung
With scarce less power than Arno's exiled
    tongue—
We who are Milton's kindred, Shakspere's
    heirs.
The prize of lyric victory who shall gain
If ours be not the laurel, ours the palm ?
More than the froth and flotsam of the Seine,
More than your Hugo-flare against the night,
And more than Weimar's proud elaborate
    calm,
One flash of Byron's lightning, Wordsworth's
    light.

The Lute-Player.

SHE was a lady great and splendid,
  I was a minstrel in her halls.
A warrior like a prince attended
  Stayed his steed by the castle walls.

Far had he fared to gaze upon her.
  " O rest thee now, Sir Knight," she said.
The warrior wooed, the warrior won her,
  In time of snowdrops they were wed.
I made sweet music in his honour,
  And longed to strike him dead.

I passed at midnight from her portal,
  Throughout the world till death I rove :
Ah, let me make this lute immortal
  With rapture of my hate and love !

The Flight of Youth.

YOUTH! ere thou be flown away,
    Surely one last boon to-day
        Thou'lt bestow—
One last light of rapture give,
Rich and lordly fugitive!
        Ere thou go.

What, thou canst not?   What, all spent?
All thy spells of ravishment
        Pow'rless now?
Gone thy magic out of date?
Gone, all gone that made thee great?—
        Follow thou!

World-Strangeness.

STRANGE the world about me lies
    Never yet familiar grown—
Still disturbs me with surprise,
    Haunts me like a face half known.

In this house with starry dome,
    Floored with gemlike plains and seas,
Shall I never feel at home,
    Never wholly be at ease?

On from room to room I stray,
    Yet my Host can ne'er espy,
And I know not to this day
    Whether guest or captive I.

So, between the starry dome
    And the floor of plains and seas,
I have never felt at home,
    Never wholly been at ease.

When Birds were Songless.

WHEN birds were songless on the bough
　　　　I heard thee sing.
The world was full of winter, thou
　　　　Wert full of spring.

To-day the world's heart feels anew
　　　　The vernal thrill,
And thine beneath the rueful yew
　　　　Is wintry chill.

On Landor's "Hellenics."

COME hither, who grow cloyed to surfeiting
   With lyric draughts o'ersweet, from rills
      that rise
On Hybla not Parnassus mountain : come
With beakers rinsed of the dulcifluous wave
Hither, and see a magic miracle
Of happiest science, the bland Attic skies
True-mirrored by an English well ;—no stream
Whose heaven-belying surface makes the stars
Reel, with its restless idiosyncrasy ;
But well unstirred, save when at times it takes
Tribute of lover's eyelids, and at times
Bubbles with laughter of some sprite below.

To a Friend

Chafing at the enforced Idleness of Interrupted Health.

SOON may the edict lapse, that on you lays
    This dire compulsion of infertile days,
This hardest penal toil, reluctant rest !
Meanwhile I count you eminently blest,
Happy from labours heretofore well done,
Happy in tasks auspiciously begun.
For they are blest that have not much to rue—
That have not oft mis-heard the prompter's
    cue,
Stammered and stumbled and the wrong parts
    played,
And life a Tragedy of Errors made.

England to Ireland.

(FEBRUARY, 1888.)

SPOUSE whom my sword in the olden time
    won me,
   Winning me hatred more sharp than a
     sword—
Mother of children who hiss at or shun me,
   Curse or revile me, and hold me abhorred—
Heiress of anger that nothing assuages,
   Mad for the future, and mad from the
     past—
Daughter of all the implacable ages,
   Lo, let us turn and be lovers at last !

Lovers whom tragical sin hath made equal,
   One in transgression and one in remorse.
Bonds may be severed, but what were the
     sequel ?
   Hardly shall amity come of divorce.

Let the dead Past have a royal entombing,
    O'er it the Future built white for a fane !
I that am haughty from much overcoming
    Sue to thee, supplicate—nay, is it vain ?

Hate and mistrust are the children of blind-
        ness,—
    Could we but see one another, 'twere
        well !
Knowledge is sympathy, charity, kindness,
    Ignorance only is maker of hell.
Could we but gaze for an hour, for a minute,
    Deep in each other's unfaltering eyes,
Love were begun—for that look would begin
        it—
    Born in the flash of a mighty surprise.

Then should the ominous night-bird of Error,
    Scared by a sudden irruption of day,
Flap his maleficent wings, and in terror
    Flit to the wilderness, dropping his prey.
Then should we, growing in strength and in
        sweetness,
    Fusing to one indivisible soul,
Dazzle the world with a splendid completeness,
    Mightily single, immovably whole.

Thou, like a flame when the stormy winds
    fan it,
  ·I, like a rock to the elements bare,—
Mixed by love's magic, the fire and the
    granite,
  Who should compete with us, what should
    compare ?
Strong with a strength that no fate might
    dissever,
  One with a oneness no force could divide,
So were we married and mingled for ever,
  Lover with lover, and bridegroom with
    bride.

The Glimpse.

JUST for a day you crossed my life's dull track,
    Put my ignobler dreams to sudden shame,
Went your bright way, and left me to fall back
    On my own world of poorer deed and aim ;

To fall back on my meaner world, and feel
    Like one who, dwelling 'mid some smoke-
        dimmed town,—
In a brief pause of labour's sullen wheel,—
    'Scaped from the street's dead dust and
        factory's frown,—

In stainless daylight saw the pure seas roll,
    Saw mountains pillaring the perfect sky :
Then journeyed home, to carry in his soul
    The torment of the difference till he die.

The Raven's Shadow.

SEABIRD, elemental sprite,
    Moulded of the sun and spray—
Raven, dreary flake of night
    Drifting in the eye of day—
What in common have ye two
Meeting 'twixt the blue and blue?

Thou to eastward carriest
    The keen savour of the foam,—
Thou dost bear unto the west
    Fragrance from thy woody home,
Where perchance a house is thine
Odorous of the oozy pine.

Eastward thee thy proper cares,
    Things of mighty moment, call ;
Thee to westward thine affairs
    Summon, weighty matters all :
I, where land and sea contest,
    Watch you eastward, watch you west,

Till, in snares of fancy caught,
  Mystically changed ye seem,
And the bird becomes a thought,
  And the thought becomes a dream,
And the dream, outspread on high,
Lords it o'er the abject sky.

Surely I have known before
  Phantoms of the shapes ye be—
Haunters of another shore
  'Leaguered by another sea.
There my wanderings night and morn
Reconcile me to the bourn.

There the bird of happy wings
  Wafts the ocean-news I crave ;
Rumours of an isle he brings
  Gemlike on the golden wave :
But the baleful beak and plume
Scatter immelodious gloom.

Though the flowers be faultless made,
  Perfectly to live and die—
Though the bright clouds bloom and fade
  Flowerlike 'midst a meadowy sky—
Where this raven roams forlorn
Veins of midnight flaw the morn.

He not less will croak and croak
   As he ever caws and caws,
Till the starry dance be broke,
   Till the sphery præan pause,
And the universal chime
Falter out of tune and time.

Coils the labyrinthine sea
   Duteous to the lunar will,
But some discord stealthily
   Vexes the world-ditty still,
And the bird that caws and caws
Clasps creation with his claws.

A Child's Hair.

A LETTER from abroad.   I tear
  Its sheathing open, unaware
What treasure gleams within ; and there—
    Like bird from cage—
Flutters a curl of golden hair
    Out of the page.

From such a frolic head 'twas shorn !
('Tis but five years since he was born.)
Not sunlight scampering over corn
    Were merrier thing.
A child ?   A fragment of the morn,
    A piece of Spring !

Surely an ampler, fuller day
Than drapes our English skies with grey—
A deeper light, a richer ray
    Than here we know—
To this bright tress have given away
    Their living glow.

For Willie dwells where gentian flowers
Make mimic sky in mountain bowers ;
And vineyards steeped in ardent hours
　　Slope to the wave
Where storied Chillon's tragic towers
　　Their bases lave ;

And over piny tracts of Vaud
The rose of eve steals up the snow ;
And on the waters far below
　　Strange sails like wings
Half-bodilessly come and go,
　　Fantastic things ;

And tender night falls like a sigh
On *châlets* low and *châteaux* high ;
And the far cataract's voice comes nigh,
　　Where no man hears ;
And spectral peaks impale the sky
　　On silver spears.

Ah, Willie, whose dissevered tress
Lies in my hand !—may you possess
At least one sovereign happiness,
　　Ev'n to your grave ;
One boon than which I ask naught less,
　　Naught greater crave :

May cloud and mountain, lake and vale,
Never to you be trite or stale
As unto souls whose wellsprings fail
    Or flow defiled,
Till Nature's happiest fairy-tale
    Charms not her child !

For when the spirit waxes numb,
Alien and strange these shows become,
And stricken with life's tedium
    The streams run dry,
The choric spheres themselves are dumb,
    And dead the sky,—

Dead as to captives grown supine,
Chained to their task in sightless mine :
Above, the bland day smiles benign,
    Birds carol free,
In thunderous throes of life divine
    Leaps the glad sea ;

But they—their day and night are one.
What is 't to them, that rivulets run,
Or what concern of theirs the sun ?
    It seems as though
Their business with these things was done
    Ages ago :

Only, at times, each dulled heart feels
That somewhere, sealed with hopeless seals,
The unmeaning heaven about him reels,
  And he lies hurled
Beyond the roar of all the wheels
  Of all the world.

. . . . . .

On what strange track one's fancies fare !
To eyeless night in sunless lair
'Tis a far cry from Willie's hair ;
  And here it lies—
Human, yet something which can ne'er
  Grow sad and wise :

Which, when the head where late it lay
In life's grey dusk itself is grey,
And when the curfew of life's day
  By death is tolled,
Shall forfeit not the auroral ray
  And eastern gold.

Ireland.

(DECEMBER 1, 1890.)

IN the wild and lurid desert, in the thunder-
    travelled ways,
'Neath the night that ever hurries to the dawn
    that still delays,
There she clutches at illusions, and she seeks
    a phantom goal
With the unattaining passion that consumes
    the unsleeping soul :
And calamity enfolds her, like the shadow of
    a ban,
And the niggardness of Nature makes the
    misery of man :
And in vain the hand is stretched to lift her,
    stumbling in the gloom,
While she follows the mad fen-fire that con-
    ducts her to her doom.

Epigrams.

Epigrams.

'TIS human fortune's happiest height to be
    A spirit melodious, lucid, poised, and
        whole ;
Second in order of felicity
    I hold it, to have walk'd with such a soul.

The statue—Buonarroti said—doth wait,
Thrall'd in the block, for me to emancipate.
The poem—saith the poet—wanders free
Till I betray it to captivity.

To keep in sight Perfection, and adore
    The vision, is the artist's best delight ;
His bitterest pang, that he can ne'er do more
    Than keep her long'd-for loveliness in sight.

If Nature be a phantasm as thou say'st
   A splendid fiction and prodigious dream,
To reach the real and true I'll make no haste,
   More than content with worlds that only
      seem.

The Poet gathers fruit from every tree,
Yea, grapes from thorns and figs from thistles
      he.
Pluck'd by his hand, the basest weed that
      grows
Towers to a lily, reddens to a rose.

Brook, from whose bridge the wandering idler
      peers
   To watch thy small fish dart or cool floor
      shine,
I would that bridge whose arches all are years
   Spann'd not a less transparent wave than
      thine !

To Art we go as to a well, athirst,
   And see our shadow 'gainst its mimic skies,
But in its depth must plunge and be im-
    mersed
   To clasp the naiad Truth where low she
    lies.

In youth the artist voweth lover's vows
To Art, in manhood maketh her his spouse.
Well if her charms yet hold for him such joy
As when he craved some boon and she was
    coy !

Immured in sense, with fivefold bonds con-
    fined,
   Rest we content if whispers from the stars
In waftings of the incalculable wind
   Come blown at midnight through our
    prison-bars.

LOVE, like a bird, hath perch'd upon a spray
  For thee and me to hearken what he sings.
Contented, he forgets to fly away ;
  But hush ! . . . remind not Eros of his
    wings.

———

THINK not thy wisdom can illume away
The ancient tanglement of night and day.
Enough, to acknowledge both, and both
        revere :
They see not clearliest who see all things
    clear.

———

IN mid whirl of the dance of Time ye start,
  Start at the cold touch of Eternity,
And cast your cloaks about you, and depart :
  The minstrels pause not in their minstrelsy.

THE beasts in field are glad, and have not wit
   To know why leapt their hearts when spring-
     time shone.
Man looks at his own bliss, considers it,
   Weighs it with curious fingers; and 'tis
     gone.

MOMENTOUS to himself as I to me
   Hath each man been that ever woman bore;
Once, in a lightning-flash of sympathy,
   I *felt* this truth, an instant, and no more.

THE gods man makes he breaks; proclaims
     them each
   Immortal, and himself outlives them all:
But whom he set not up he cannot reach
   To shake His cloud-dark sun-bright pedestal.

THE children romp within the graveyard's
    pale ;
The lark sings o'er a madhouse, or a gaol ;—
Such nice antitheses of perfect poise
Chance in her curious rhetoric employs.

***

OUR lithe thoughts gambol close to God's
    abyss,
Children whose home is by the precipice.
Fear not thy little ones shall o'er it fall :
Solid, though viewless, is the girdling wall.

***

LIVES there whom pain hath evermore pass'd
    by
And Sorrow shunn'd with an averted eye ?
Him do thou pity, him above the rest,
Him of all hapless mortals most unbless'd.

SAY what thou wilt, the young are happy
    never.
Give me bless'd Age, beyond the fire and
    fever,—
Past the delight that shatters, hope that stings,
And eager flutt'ring of life's ignorant wings.

——— ——

ONWARD the chariot of the Untarrying moves ;
    Nor day divulges him nor night conceals ;
Thou hear'st the echo of unreturning hooves
    And thunder of irrevocable wheels.

———————

A DEFT musician does the breeze become
    Whenever an Æolian harp it finds :
Hornpipe and hurdygurdy both are dumb
    Unto the most musicianly of winds.

I FOLLOW Beauty ; of her train am I :
     Beauty whose voice is earth and sea and air ;
Who serveth, and her hands for all things ply ;
     Who reigneth, and her throne is everywhere.

TOILING and yearning, 'tis man's doom to see
     No perfect creature fashion'd of his hands.
Insulted by a flower's immaculacy,
     And mock'd at by the flawless stars he
     stands.

FOR metaphors of man we search the skies,
     And find our allegory in all the air.
We gaze on Nature with Narcissus-eyes,
     Enamour'd of our shadow everywhere.

ONE music maketh its occult abode
  In all things scatter'd from great Beauty's
    hand ;
And evermore the deepest words of God
  Are yet the easiest to understand.

ENOUGH of mournful melodies, my lute !
Be henceforth joyous, or be henceforth mute.
Song's breath is wasted when it does but fan
The smouldering infelicity of man.

I PLUCK'D this flower, O brighter flower, for
    thee,
There where the river dies into the sea.
To kiss it the wild west wind hath made free :
Kiss it thyself and give it back to me.

To be as this old elm full loth were I,
 That shakes in the autumn storm its palsied
  head.
Hewn by the weird last woodman let me lie
 Ere the path rustle with my foliage shed.

———

His rhymes the poet flings at all men's feet,
 And whoso will may trample on his rhymes.
Should Time let die a song that's true and
  sweet,
 The singer's loss were more than match'd
  by Time's.

On Longfellow's Death.

No puissant singer he, whose silence grieves
   To-day the great West's tender heart and
      strong ;
No singer vast of voice : yet one who leaves
   His native air the sweeter for his song.

Byron the Voluptuary.

Too avid of earth's bliss, he was of those
   Whom Delight flies because they give her
      chase.
Only the odour of her wild hair blows
   Back in their faces hungering for her face.

ANTONY AT ACTIUM.

HE holds a dubious balance :—yet *that* scale,
Whose freight the world is, surely shall pre-
    vail ?
No ; Cleopatra droppeth into *this*
One counterpoising orient sultry kiss.

ART.

THE thousand painful steps at last are trod,
   At last the temple's difficult door we win ;
But perfect on his pedestal, the god
   Freezes us hopeless when we enter in.

KEATS.

HE dwelt with the bright gods of elder time,
  On earth and in their cloudy haunts above.
He loved them : and in recompense sublime,
  The gods, alas ! gave him their fatal love.

AFTER READING " TAMBURLAINE THE GREAT."

YOUR Marlowe's page I close, my Shakspere's
    ope.
  How welcome—after gong and cymbal's
    din—
The continuity, the long slow slope
  And vast curves of the gradual violin !

Shelley and Harriet Westbrook.

A star look'd down from heaven and loved a
    flower
Grown in earth's garden—loved it for an hour :

Let eyes that trace his orbit in the spheres
Refuse not, to a ruin'd rosebud, tears.

The Play of "King Lear."

Here Love the slain with Love the slayer
    lies ;
    Deep drown'd are both in the same sunless
      pool.
Up from its depths that mirror thundering
    skies
    Bubbles the wan mirth of the mirthless
      Fool.

To a Poet.

Time, the extortioner, from richest beauty
Takes heavy toll and wrings rapacious duty.
Austere of feature if thou carve thy rhyme,
Perchance 'twill pay the lesser tax to Time.

— —

The Year's Minstrelsy.

Spring, the low prelude of a lordlier song :
  Summer, a music without hint of death :
Autumn, a cadence lingeringly long :
  Winter, a pause ;—the Minstrel-Year takes
    breath.

The Ruined Abbey.

Flower-fondled, clasp'd in ivy's close caress,
   It seems allied with Nature, yet apart :—
Of wood's and wave's insensate loveliness
   The glad, sad, tranquil, passionate, human
     heart.

Michelangelo's "Moses."

The captain's might, and mystery of the
   seer—
Remoteness of Jehovah's colloquist,
Nearness of man's heaven-advocate—are here :
   Alone Mount Nebo's harsh foreshadow is
     miss'd.

THE ALPS.

ADIEU, white brows of Europe! sovereign
 brows,
 That wear the sunset for a golden tiar.
With me in memory shall your phantoms
 house
 For ever, whiter than yourselves, and
 higher.

THE CATHEDRAL SPIRE.

IT soars like hearts of hapless men who dare
 To sue for gifts the gods refuse to allot ;
Who climb for ever toward they know not
 where,
 Baffled for ever by they know not what.

AN EPITAPH.

His friends he loved.   His fellest earthly foes—
    Cats—I believe he did but feign to hate.
My hand will miss the insinuated nose,
    Mine eyes the tail that wagg'd contempt at
        Fate.

THE METROPOLITAN UNDERGROUND RAILWAY.

HERE were a goodly place wherein to die ;—
    Grown latterly to sudden change averse,
All violent contrasts fain avoid would I
    On passing from this world into a worse.

ON SEEING THE TOMB OF INFANT BROTHERS TWIN-BORN.

MATES of the cradle, fellows of the grave,
  A handbreadth parts them in the mould
    below ;
Whom, had they lived, perhaps the estranging
    wave,
  Or hate—or love—had sunder'd wide enow.

A MAIDEN'S EPITAPH.

SHE dwelt among us till the flowers, 'tis said,
  Grew jealous of her : with precipitate feet,
As loth to wrong them unawares, she fled.
  Earth is less fragrant now, and heaven more
    sweet.

To Professor Dowden.

·· To Professor Dowden,

ON RECEIVING FROM HIM A COPY OF
"THE LIFE OF SHELLEY."

FIRST, ere I slake my hunger, let me thank
  The giver of the feast. For feast it is,
Though of ethereal, translunary fare—
His story who pre-eminently of men
Seemed nourished upon starbeams and the stuff
Of rainbows, and the tempest, and the foam ;
Who hardly brooked on his impatient soul
The fleshly trammels ; whom at last the sea
Gave to the fire, from whose wild arms the
  winds
Took him, and shook him broadcast to the
  world.

In my young days of fervid poesy
He drew me to him with his strange far
  light,—
He held me in a world all clouds and gleams,
And vasty phantoms, where ev'n Man himself
Moved like a phantom 'mid the clouds and
  gleams.

Anon the Earth recalled me, and a voice
Murmuring of dethroned divinities
And dead times deathless upon sculptured
    urn—
And Philomela's long-descended pain
Flooding the night—and maidens of romance
To whom asleep St. Agnes' love-dreams
    come—
Awhile constrained me to a sweet duresse
And thraldom, lapping me in high content,
Soft as the bondage of white amorous arms.
And then a third voice, long unheeded—
    held
Claustral and cold, and dissonant and tame—
Found me at last with ears to hear.   It sang
Of lowly sorrows and familiar joys,
Of simple manhood, artless womanhood,
And childhood fragrant as the limpid morn ;
And from the homely matter nigh at hand
Ascending and dilating, it disclosed
Spaces and avenues, calm heights and breadths
Of vision, whence I saw each blade of
    grass
With roots that groped about eternity,
And in each drop of dew upon each blade
The mirror of the inseparable All.

The first voice, then the second, in their turns
Had sung me captive. This voice sang me
  free.
Therefore, above all vocal sons of men,
Since him whose sightless eyes saw hell and
    heaven,
To Wordsworth be my homage, thanks, and
    love.
Yet dear is Keats, a lucid presence, great
With somewhat of a glorious soullessness.
And dear, and great with an excess of soul,
Shelley, the hectic flamelike rose of verse,
All colour, and all odour, and all bloom,
Steeped in the noonlight, glutted with the
    sun,
But somewhat lacking root in homely earth,
Lacking such human moisture as bedews
His not less starward stem of song, who, rapt
Not less in glowing vision, yet retained
His clasp of the prehensible, retained
The warm touch of the world that lies to
    hand,
Not in vague dreams of man forgetting men,
Nor in vast morrows losing the to-day ;
Who trusted nature, trusted fate, nor found
An Ogre, sovereign on the throne of things ;

Who felt the incumbence of the unknown, yet
    bore
Without resentment the Divine reserve ;
Who suffered not his spirit to dash itself
Against the crags and wavelike break in spray,
But 'midst the infinite tranquillities
Moved tranquil, and henceforth, by Rotha
    stream
And Rydal's mountain-mirror, and where
    flows
Yarrow thrice sung or Duddon to the sea,
And wheresoe'er man's heart is thrilled by
    tones
Struck from man's lyric heartstrings, shall
    survive.

The Gresham Press,

UNWIN BROTHERS,

CHILWORTH AND LONDON.